Gilbert the Prize Winning Pig

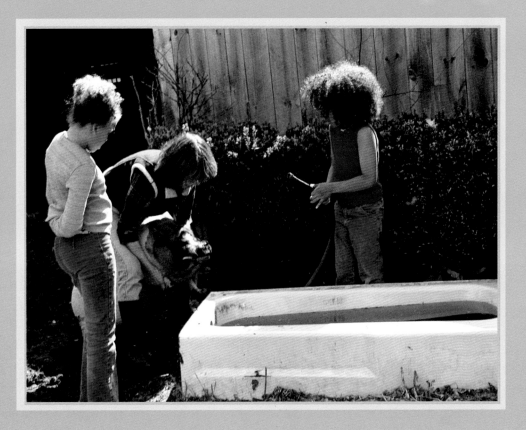

by Michèle Dufresne

PIONEER VALLEY EDUCATIONAL PRESS, INC.

"No, Gilbert, no!"

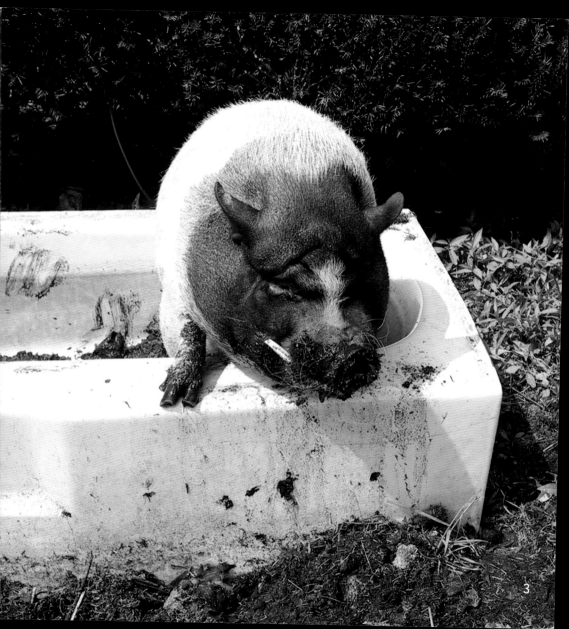

"No, no, no!"

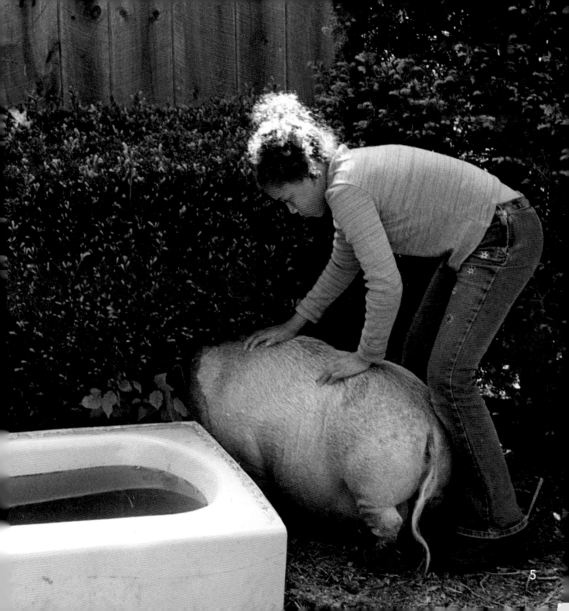

"No! No! Gilbert, no!"

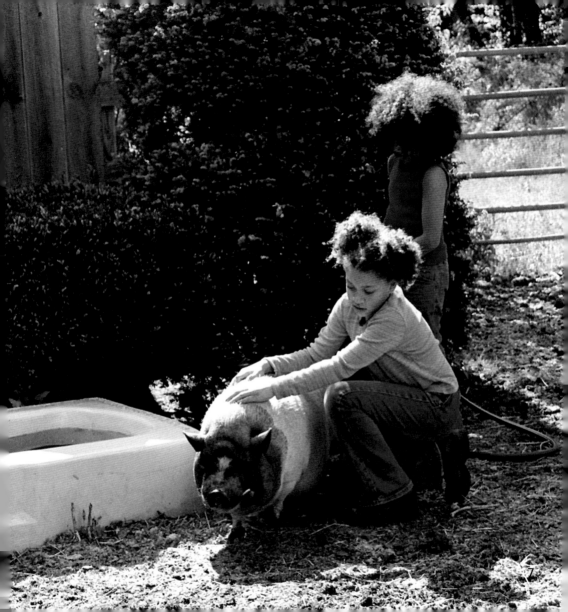

"No, Gilbert, no!

Stop!"

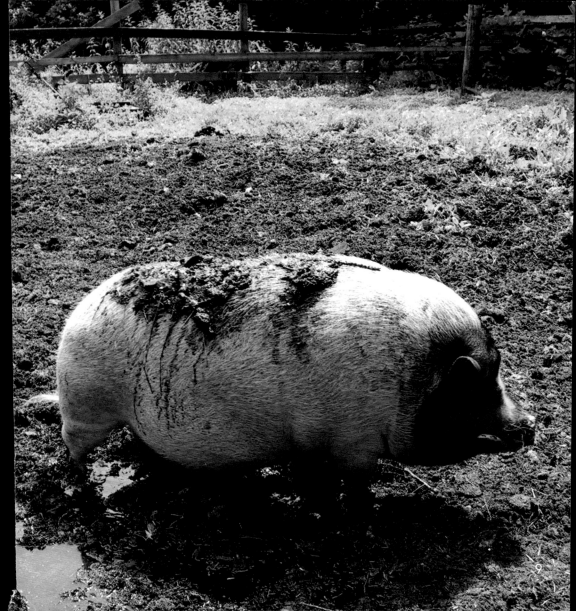

"Yes, yes, yes!"

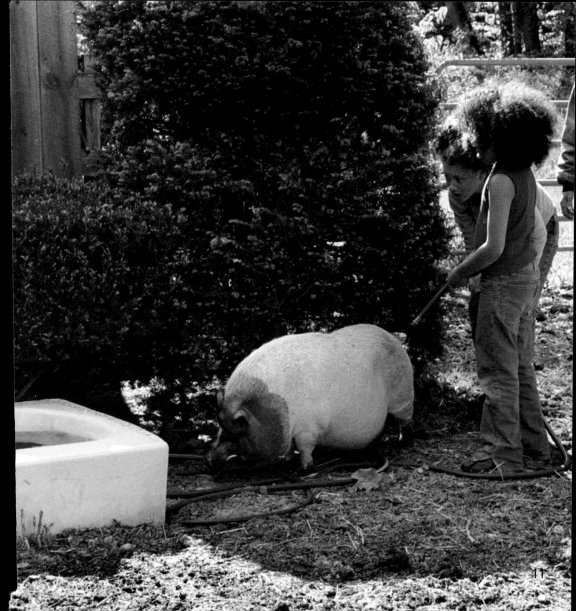

"Yes, Gilbert, yes!"

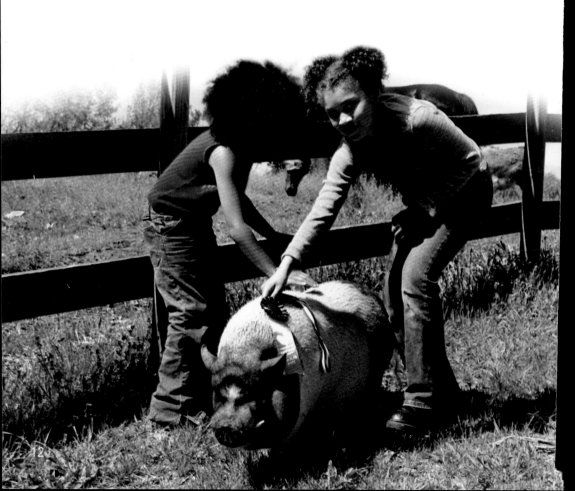